[redacted]

Millions
of
MAXES

by Meg WOLITZER

illustrated by MICAH Player

DIAL BOOKS FOR YOUNG READERS

Max's room had his name all over it.
It was on the wall.
It was on the floor.
It was even on the ceiling.

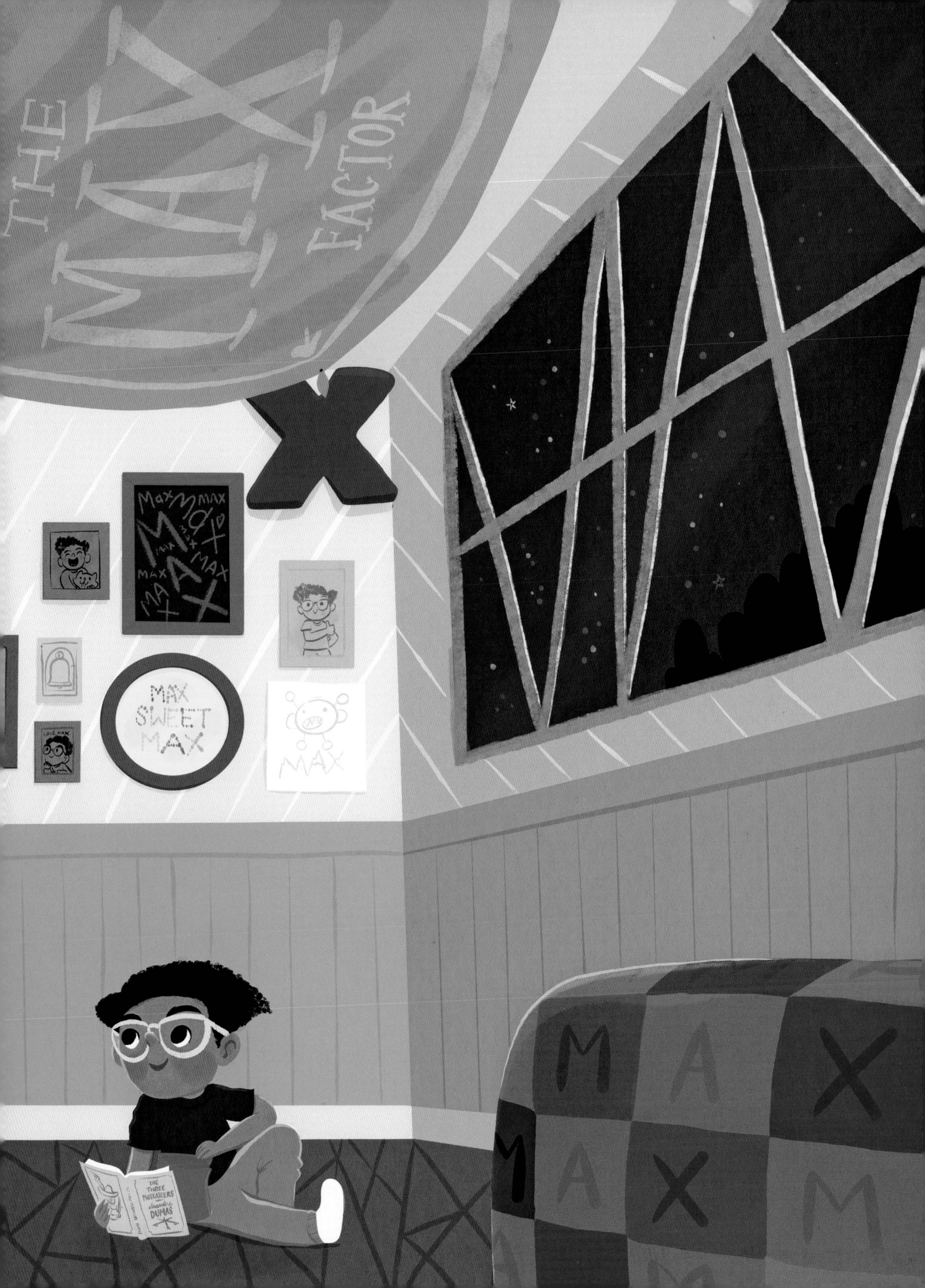
THE MAX FACTOR
MAX SWEET MAX
MAX
LOVE MAX
THE THREE MUSKETEERS
Alexandre DUMAS

"Time for bed, one and only Max,"
his parents said each night.

They took away his MAX cup.
They turned on his MAX night-light.
They tucked him in under his MAX blanket.

In the dark, Max dreamed the dreams of the one and only Max.

Then one day, Dad took him to the playground.

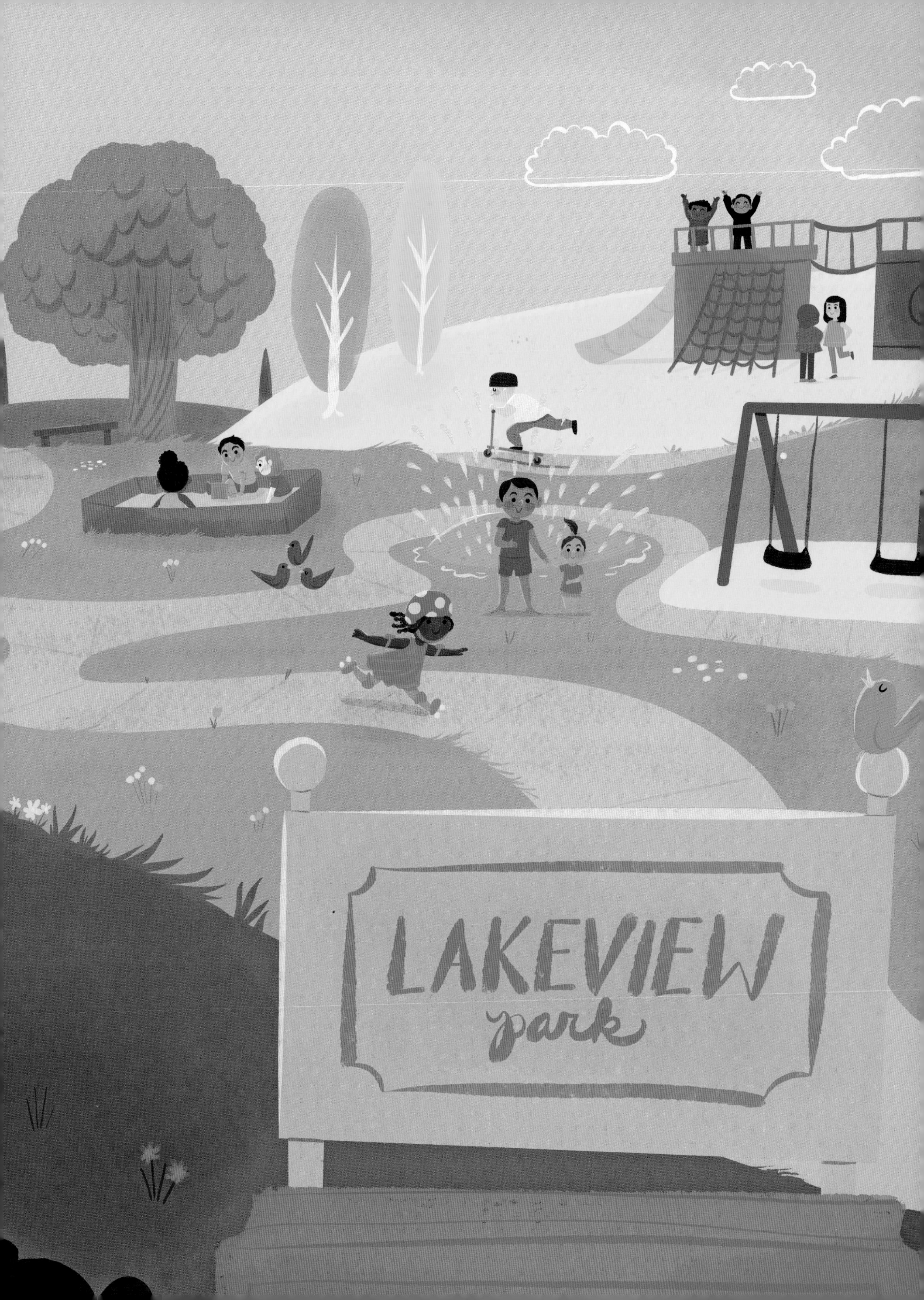
LAKEVIEW
park

Max ran all over.
He was extremely fast.

He rushed around
the sandbox.

He raced past the pigeons.

He roared right through the sprinkler.

Then he heard:

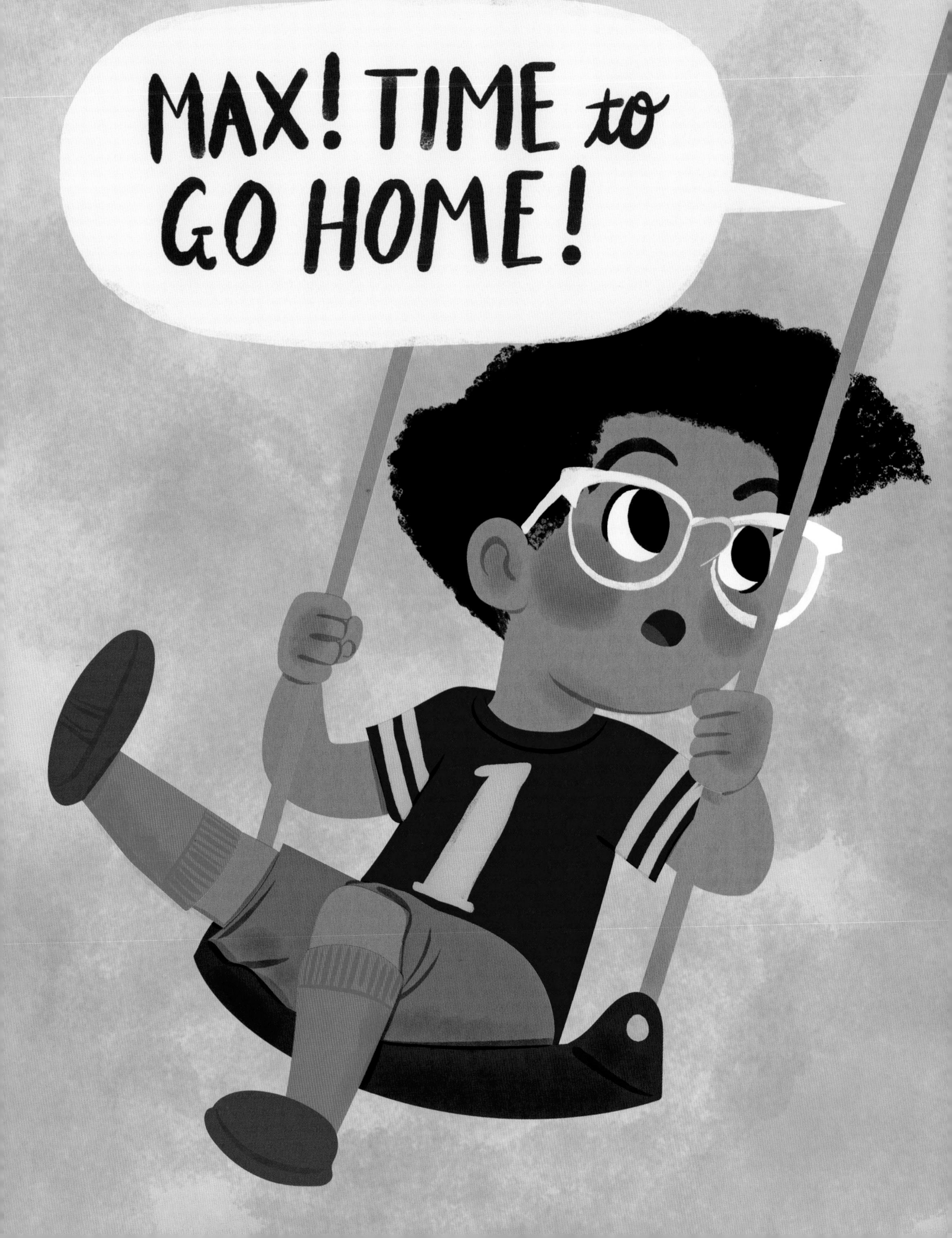
MAX! TIME to GO HOME!

"I'm coming!" shouted the one and only Max, and he ran toward the benches.

But then someone else shouted:

I'M COMING!

And someone else shouted:

Max whirled around. Two kids were heading his way, one on a scooter and one on roller skates.

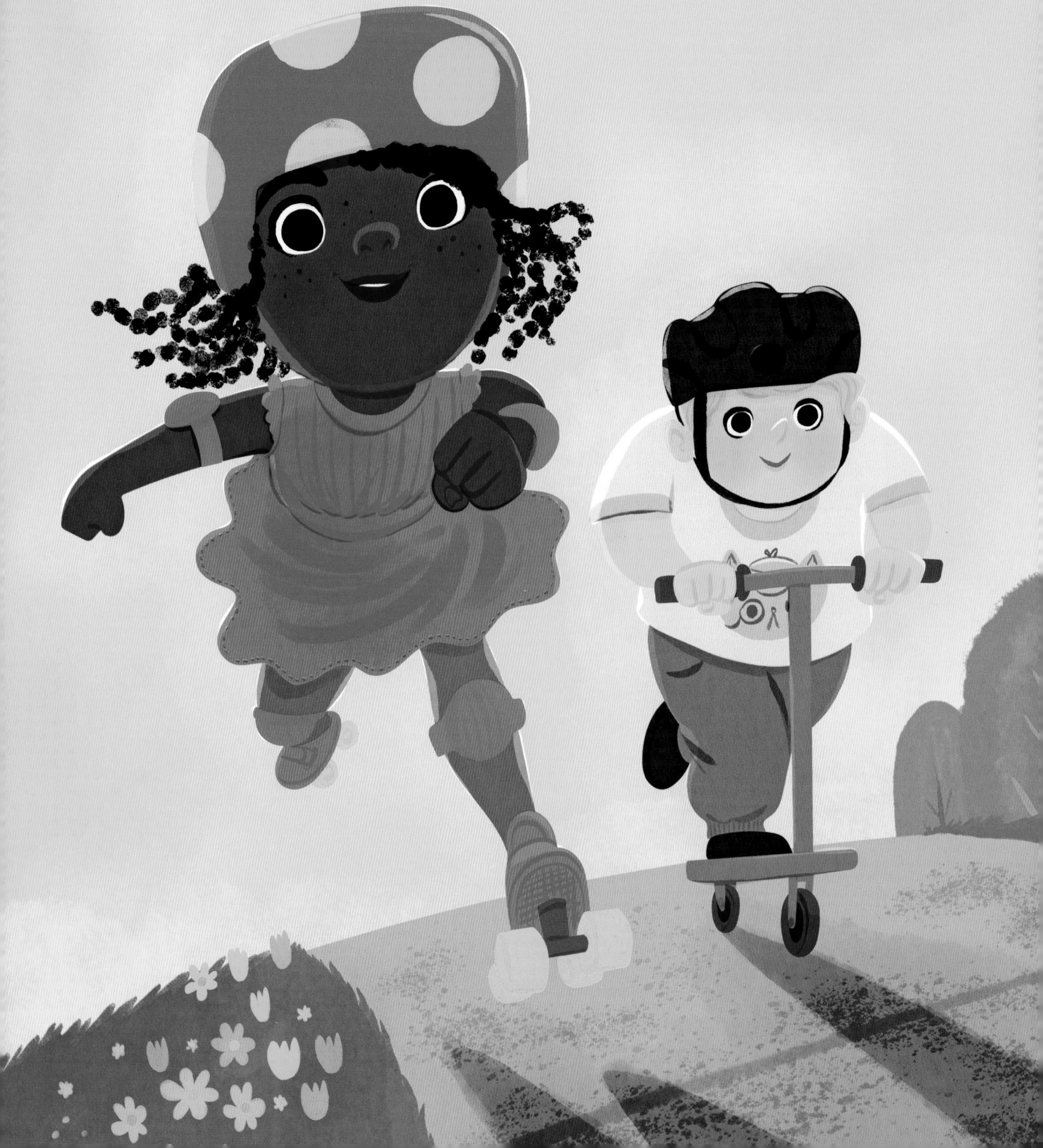

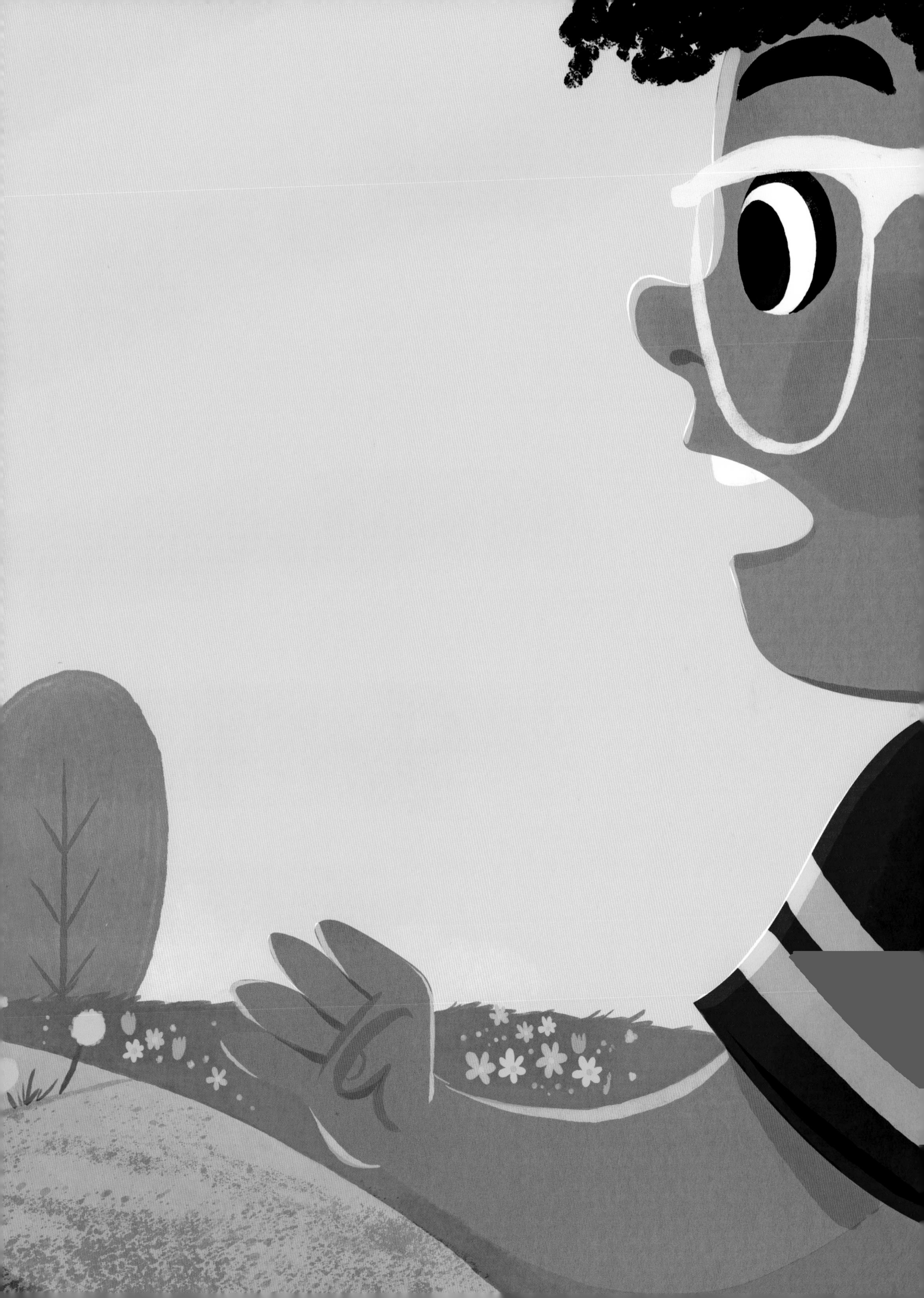

THERE you are, MAX. ARE you READY to GO?

a dad said to the kid on skates.

"You're Max?" asked the one and only Max.
She nodded.
"But *I'm* Max," he said.

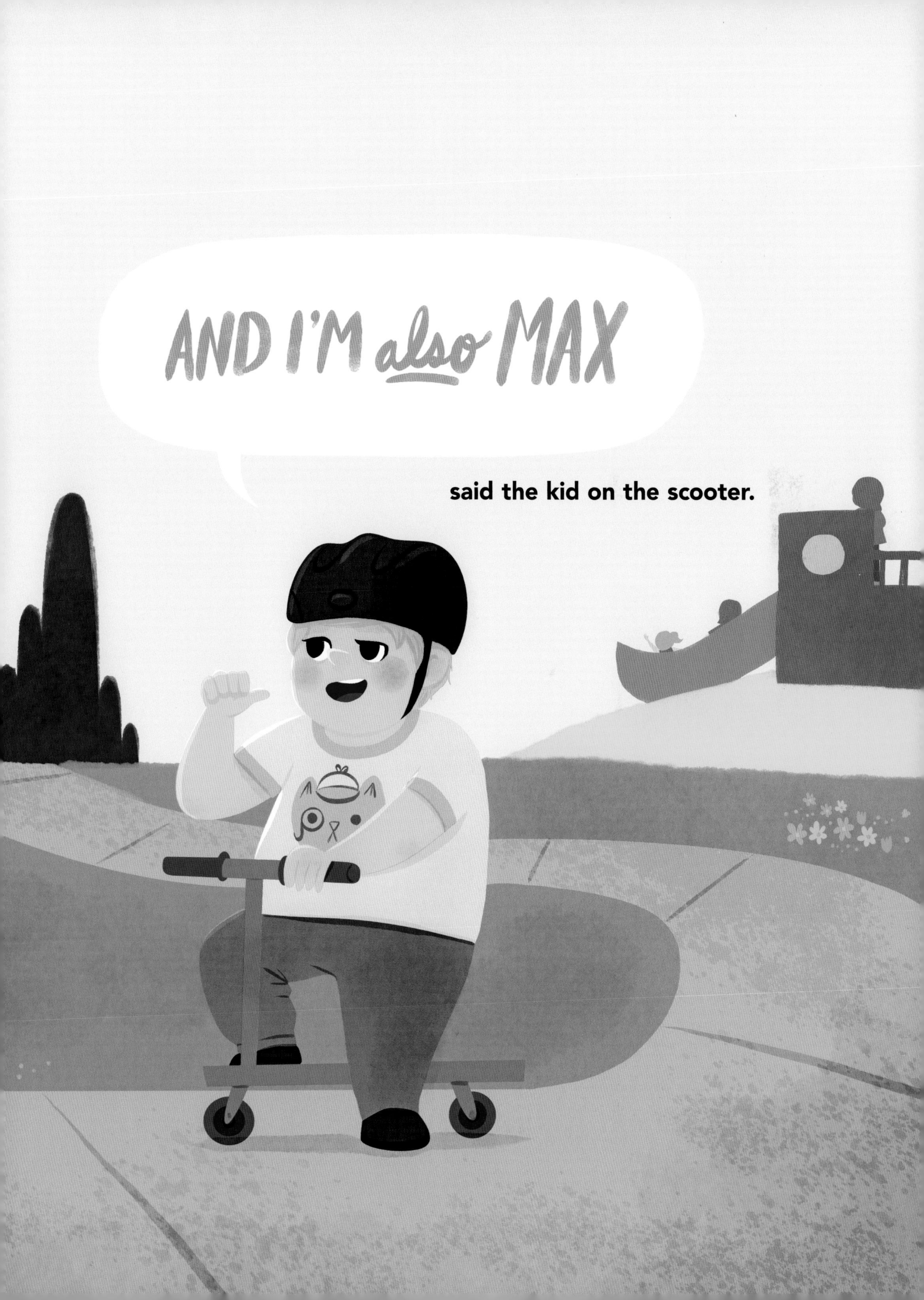
AND I'M also MAX

said the kid on the scooter.

"WHAT IS GOING ON HERE?"
asked the one and only Max.
He sat down next to his dad, who just
kept on reading his book, as if nothing
bad had happened.

How many Maxes were in the world?

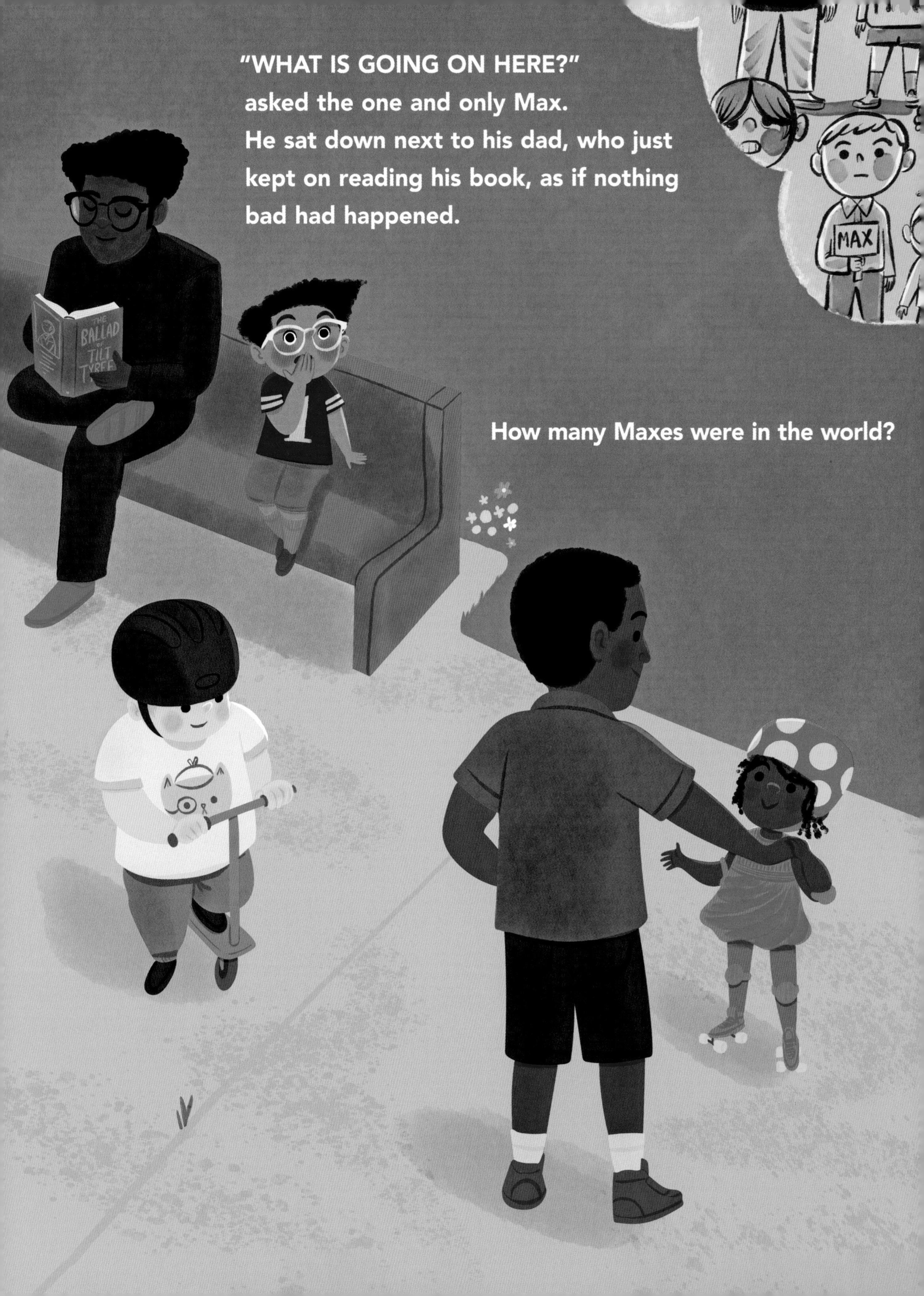
BALLAD
TILT
MAX

Maybe there were hundreds of them.
Or thousands. There could even be...
MILLIONS of Maxes.

And maybe all of those Maxes thought that
they were the one and only Max.

But they weren't.

I am NOT the one and only Max, thought Max.
And I never, ever was.
He could not believe it.

Max on skates said to her dad, "Wait, we can't leave yet! I can't find my pink pine cone."

"Sorry, Max," said her dad. "We have to get going. You can paint another pine cone at home."

"But I like that one."

Max on the scooter said, "I can help you look for it."

And Max who was no longer
the one and only Max said,
"I can help too."

"Can we, Dad?" asked Max on skates.
"Please?"
"Okay," said her dad. "Five minutes."

So all the Maxes were off.
First they ran and skated and scootered.

Then one of them skated and two of them scootered.

They rushed around the sandbox.
They raced past the pigeons.
They roared right through the sprinkler.

All of them shouted,
"HAS ANYONE SEEN A PINK PINE CONE?"

"Is that it?" someone called from the top of a slide.

The Maxes screeched to a stop.

They came closer.

And closer.

Max on skates bent down to look.

There under a tree was something pink. Could it be?

She picked it up.

But it wasn't a pine cone at all.
It was a pink Ping-Pong ball.

So they kept looking,
and kept shouting,
**"HAS ANYONE SEEN
A PINK PINE CONE?"**

"Is that it?" someone called from the bottom of a seesaw.

The Maxes screeched
to a stop again.
There in the grass was
something pink.

They came closer.
And closer.

But before they could see what it was, up ran a little
white dog. It snatched the pink thing in its mouth
and raced away.

"Follow that dog!" cried the no longer one and only Max.

They scootered and skated and followed that little white dog right through the sprinkler, past the pigeons, around the sandbox, and over to a kid who was sitting on one of the benches eating a sandwich.

The dog dropped the pink thing beside her and wagged its tail.

"There you are!" the kid said, patting her dog. "What did you bring me? Oh, what a nice pink pine cone. Thank you, Max!"

"Wait a minute," said Max on the scooter.
"Your dog is named Max?"

All the Maxes started laughing.
"HO HO HO," said Max on roller skates.
"HEE HEE HEE," said Max on the scooter.
"HA HA HA," said the no longer one and only Max.

"What's so funny about the name Max?" asked the kid with the dog. "I think it's a great name."
"We do too," said all the Maxes.

Max on the scooter picked up her pink pine cone and hugged it.

PINEY! I'M SO GLAD I found YOU.

That night, Max's parents said, "Time for bed, one and only Max."
They took away his MAX cup.
They turned on his MAX night-light.
They tucked him in under his MAX blanket.
"Actually," said Max, "I'm *not* the one and only Max,
and I never was."

"Oh no? Then who are you?" asked Dad.
"The one and only Throckmorton?"
"Or maybe," said Mom, "the one and only Fred?"

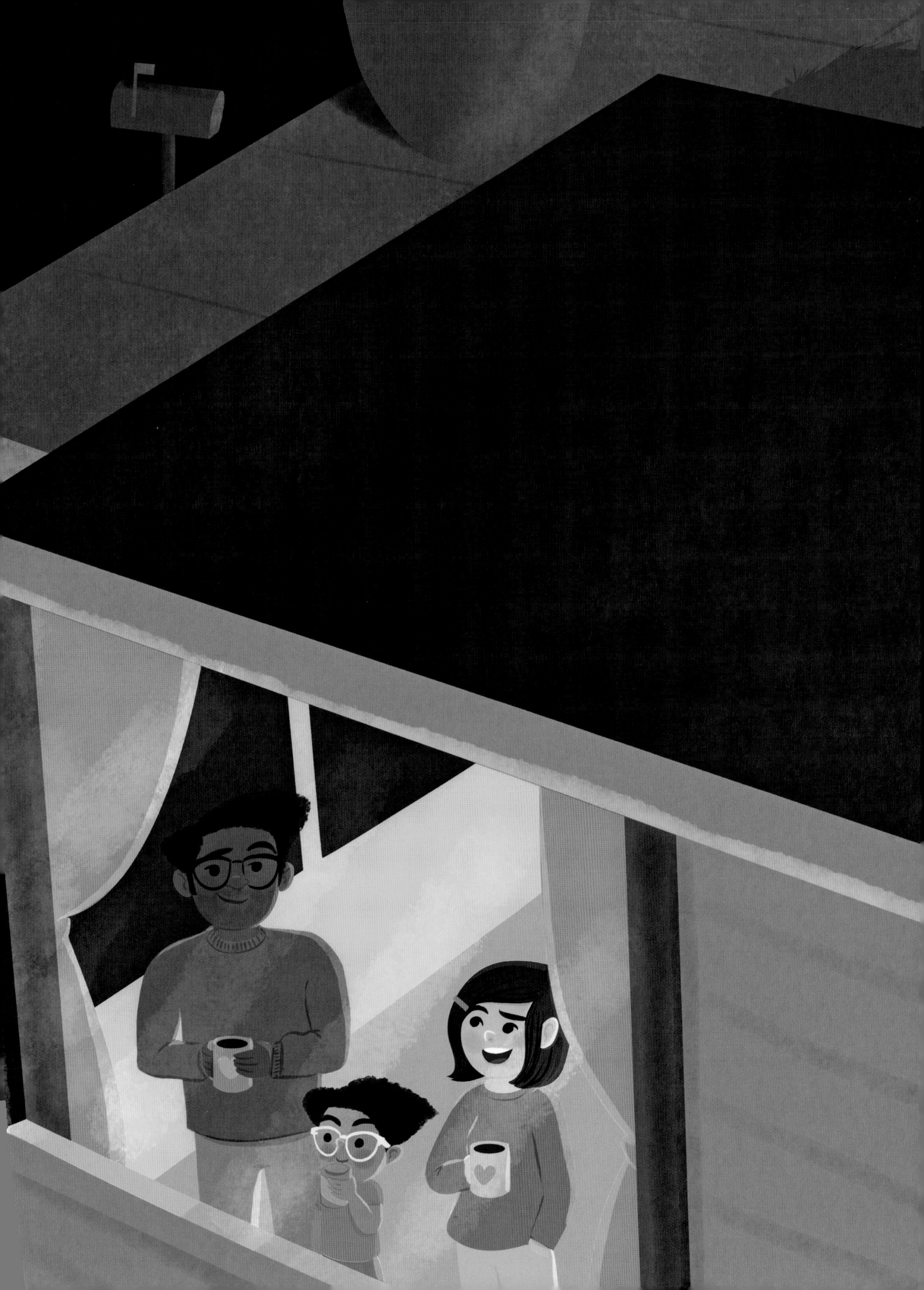

"No, just Max," said Max. "Today I met two more Maxes.
I mean three. One likes to roller skate, one likes to scooter,
and one has a tail."

"Excuse me?" said Dad. "Did you say a *tail*?"

"Yes, because he's a dog," said Max. "We all have the same name, but we're completely different. One goes HO HO HO when she laughs, one goes HEE HEE HEE. And I go HA HA HA. And that other Max probably goes WOOF WOOF WOOF.

"I might see them again at the park tomorrow," he said.

the ONE and ONLY Max ♡

"And maybe we'll meet even more Maxes," said Max.
"Hundreds of them. Thousands of them."
He closed his eyes.

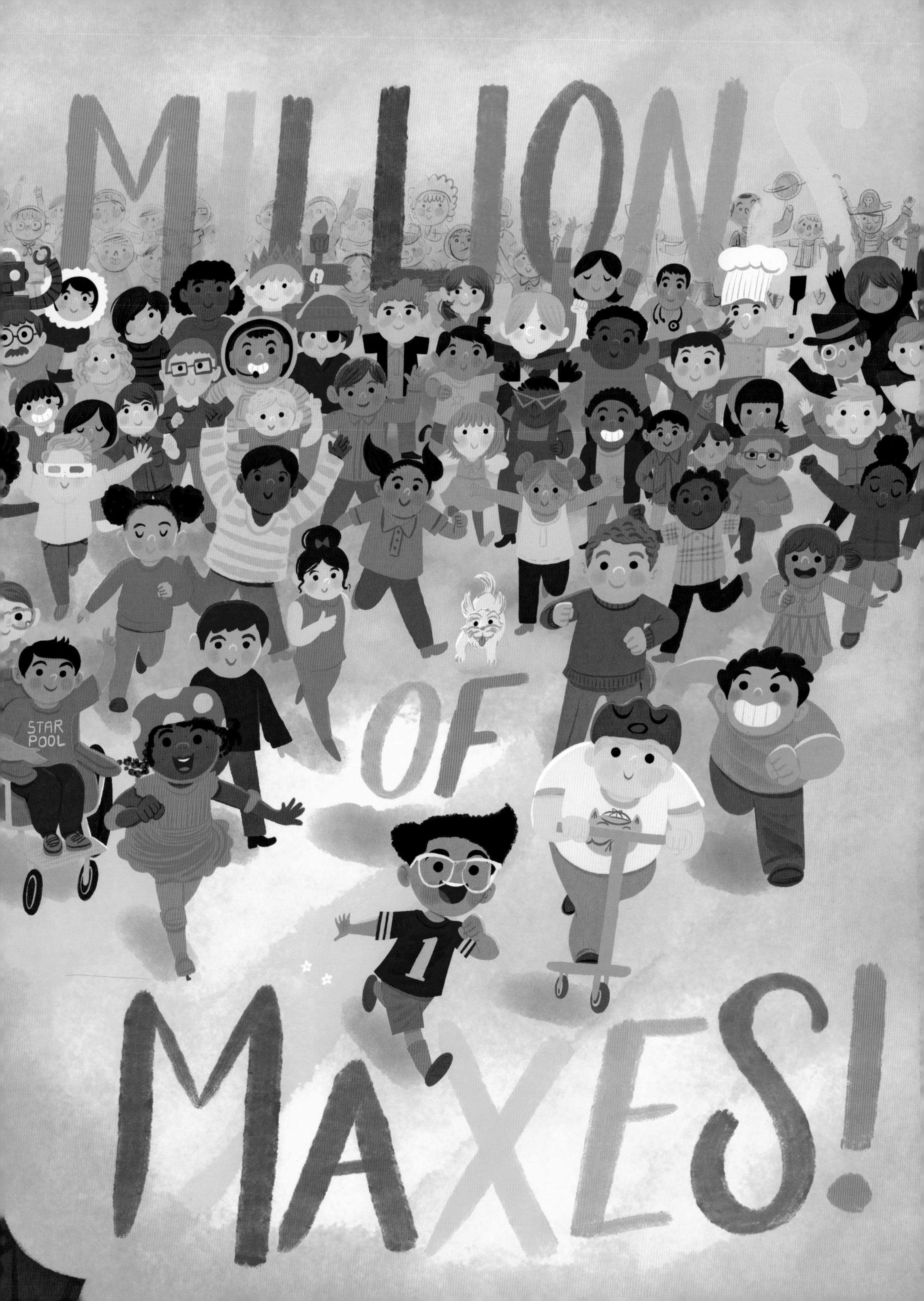
MILLIONS
OF
MAXES!
STAR POOL
1

To my mother,
who was the first to read to me
—M.W.

To my favorite Maxes, B and P
—M.P.

DIAL BOOKS FOR YOUNG READERS

An imprint of Penguin Random House LLC • New York

First published in the United States of America by Dial Books for Young Readers,
an imprint of Penguin Random House LLC, 2021

Library of Congress Cataloging-in-Publication Data is available.

The artwork for this book was painted digitally in Adobe Photoshop and Fresco
Design by Jason Henry • Manufactured in China
RRD
ISBN 9780593324110 • 10 9 8 7 6 5 4 3 2 1

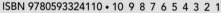